RENT
-A-
PET

RENT -A- PET

AND OTHER ANIMAL STORIES
Compiled by the Editors
of
Highlights for Children

CONTENTS

RENT -A- PET

By Jeanette D. Knapp

Sam and Nate loved Brownie the moment they saw the cute little hamster staring at them from his cage. He had fuzzy brown fur and shiny dark eyes. He looked warm and friendly and was just the right size for a third grader to hold in his hand. And best of all Brownie was on sale—only ninety-nine cents. Together they had plenty of money to buy him.

The problem was that when Sam took Brownie home, his mother said, "No pets." And when Nate took Brownie home, his mother started sneezing and sneezing and SNEEZING!

Their last hope was their teacher. Surely she would want Brownie for a class pet. "Please," Sam said. "We'll feed him every day and clean his cage."

Mrs. Winslow smiled at Nate and Sam. "I think Brownie sounds like fun," she said, "like a rent-a-pet that I don't have to worry about."

Sam would have leaped up in delight, except that Mrs. Winslow put her hand on his shoulder and asked a strange question. "Are you prepared to be philosophical if something happens to Brownie?"

Sam wasn't quite sure what Mrs. Winslow meant, but it sounded important, and sad. Sam nodded, hoping he would never have to find out what being philosophical meant.

Brownie was a big hit in the classroom. The children gathered around his cage every morning. They watched Sam and Nate take out yesterday's chewed carrots and lettuce and replace them with fresh apple slices and peanuts. Brownie stuffed the new food into his swelling cheek pouches. He dove into his wood shavings to his plastic house to bury his treasure. Then he jumped on his wheel and twirled and spun. Later, when the children were busy with their reading groups, he would snuggle into his house and nibble his food.

Before school or during rainy-day recesses, Sam and Nate would take Brownie out of the cage and hold him gently. Brownie usually squirmed to be set free. They loved feeling his wiggly nose and tickly feet.

When they cleaned the cage, they put Brownie into his clear plastic ball. When he tried to climb to the top of the ball, it rolled forward. The harder he climbed, the faster the ball rolled, with the tiny hamster inside.

One afternoon Brownie rolled all the way to the kindergarten room. The little boy who first spotted Brownie shrieked. He thought Brownie was a space monster. Sam took Brownie out of the plastic ball and held him so that each kindergartner could touch Brownie's warm fur.

On a Friday morning, a week before Thanksgiving, Sam tapped on Brownie's cage. "Guess what?" he said. "Mom said I can take you home for Thanksgiving on Tuesday. We can play all weekend."

Sam expected to see the old sock that Brownie snuggled in start to jiggle. But this morning there was no rustling.

A twinge of fear gripped his stomach. The two blocks that usually held down the wire-mesh lid were sitting beside the glass cage, not on top. Had he forgotten to put them back last night?

He lifted up the mesh top. Then he picked up the small plastic house. Brownie wasn't there. He felt all through the cedar shavings. He found hidden stores of raisins and hamster pellets. He even discovered one of the men from the Chutes and Ladders game, but no Brownie.

"Hi, Sam," Nate said. "How's Brownie?"

"He's gone," Sam whispered. If he didn't say the awful words aloud, they might not be true. "I can't find him."

"He has to be here somewhere," Nate said. On his hands and knees he felt along the bookshelf for a hidden hamster. Soon the whole class was crawling along the floor looking for Brownie in wastebaskets and behind books and chairs.

When the bell rang, Mrs. Winslow said they had to stop the search. Sam was glad she didn't ask him about being philosophical, for Sam was too close to tears to answer.

Mrs. Winslow gave Sam a note about Brownie to take to each teacher. The kindergartners were making a Thanksgiving display when Sam brought their teacher the note. She said, "Try not to worry. You know, hamsters are very clever about taking care of themselves."

But Sam couldn't help worrying. All that morning, he kept looking up from his math problems, hoping to catch a glimpse of Brownie. Brownie was so little, and he couldn't see very well. Suppose someone stepped on him?

At lunchtime Sam and Nate hunted for Brownie behind all the boxes in Mrs. Winslow's closet. But no Brownie.

Snow began falling while the class was writing in their journals that afternoon. "Suppose Brownie follows someone outside," Sam wrote. "He could get squashed when the door slams. Or he'll freeze to death in the snow. Hamsters aren't used to the cold."

On Monday Sam raced into the classroom hoping that Brownie would be there waiting, his paws and nose pressed against the glass cage. Brownie's cage was silent and empty.

That noon Sam and Nate hunted for Brownie in the first grade room. "I suppose we could get another hamster," Nate said.

"Don't say that," Sam cried. There would never be another Brownie. He wondered who was being philosophical, Nate or himself.

By Tuesday, Sam was frantic with worry. How would Brownie survive the long Thanksgiving weekend without food and water?

Around noon Mr. Kamen, the custodian, stopped by the learning center. Sam and Nate were checking behind all the books and magazines. "I can't figure it out," he said to them. "I've looked every-where for Brownie, too. And if that isn't enough," he added, "someone's been messing up the kindergarten Thanksgiving display. They've taken all the nuts and most of the apples. Kids!"

"I bet Brownie could really go for some nuts and apples right now," Nate said.

Brownie! Sam stared at his friend, and then Nate let out a whoop. Together they dashed down the hallway to the kindergarten room. The fruit and vegetable display had shrunk, and the Indian corn was half eaten.

Nate and Sam peeked behind the large display board that was leaning against the wall. There was Brownie, sleeping in a burrow of nuts and shelled corn, his head and feet snuggled between two apples.

"You're a lot smarter than we were, Brownie," Nate said as he picked up the plump hamster.

Sam felt wonderfully happy as he tickled Brownie under the chin. "When Grandpa asks me what I'm thankful for, Brownie, I'm going to have an answer this year."

The Safest Hiding Place

By Sondra Eklund

Everyone in the neighborhood knew that Sally was afraid of dogs. That made it extra hard to hide her tears as she crawled out of the mud.

She and the other neighborhood kids were playing hide-and-seek. As usual, Sally was caught first. She had been waiting on Jeremy Painter's front doorstep when it happened. The door sprang open and King, the Painters' German Shepherd, burst out.

King wasn't one to let a guest go ungreeted. He jumped toward Sally and eagerly tried to lick her face. Alarmed, Sally stepped back, not realizing she was on the edge of the porch. Splat! She landed in Mrs. Painter's petunias.

As if that weren't bad enough, Sally then saw who was holding the other end of King's leash. It was Amanda, Sally's big sister. Amanda loved dogs, no matter how big. She kept asking their parents for one of her own, but they felt that it wouldn't be fair to Sally.

So Amanda just looked at her sister scornfully as Sally picked herself out of the mud.

"He was only trying to say hello," Amanda said. "Come on, King, let's go for a walk."

Then Sally saw Jeremy, Jessica, Dennis, and Lori all coming to the base.

"What happened to you?" Lori asked.

"King knocked me down," Sally mumbled.

The other kids exchanged glances but didn't say any more.

Dennis was "It" next. He started counting and everyone scattered. Sally hesitated. She was tired of being found first. Then she had an idea. King was off with Amanda, so why couldn't she hide in the Painters' backyard? She'd never hidden there before, and no one would expect it.

The gate was unlocked, but it clattered a little when she shut it. She ducked behind a woodpile, only to find she was in plain view of anyone looking over the back fence. Next she tried the tool shed beside King's doghouse, but it was locked.

"Ready or not, here I come!" Dennis shouted.

Sally had taken too long. Her only chance now was King's doghouse.

She knelt down and started in. Phew! It reeked of dog, dust, and dirt. She shuddered. What if there were spiders?

Slowly, she crawled in. Blech! She thought she felt a spider's web brush her face.

She had almost decided it wasn't worth it when the gate clattered. To her dismay, Sally heard loud barking. Amanda's voice said, "Sorry, King, I have to go home now." The gate clattered again, and Sally's heart sank.

Right away she heard King bounding toward the doghouse. She wanted to get out, but didn't have a chance. The next thing she knew, King was right beside her.

Sally barely had room to cower against the back wall. King didn't have room to jump. He barked excitedly. He had licked her whole face before she was able to poke her head out of the doghouse.

She froze. Directly in front of her was Dennis, latching the gate behind him. If he turned around, he'd stare right at her.

Shaking, Sally ducked back into the doghouse. King started licking again where he had left off. She winced at the wet, slimy feel of his tongue all over her face.

Amanda had told her once that dogs could smell fear. Sally closed her eyes and pretended she was in bed holding her furry teddy bear. She breathed deeply.

Suddenly, King tensed. Sally heard Dennis's footsteps coming closer. In one smooth motion, King turned and sprang from the doghouse.

"Down, King! Go away! Get down!" Dennis didn't sound all that brave, either. His shouts retreated quickly. Instead of giving Sally away, King had rushed Dennis out of the yard.

When King returned to the doghouse, Sally greeted him bravely. She stroked his soft fur gingerly. His warm body cuddled against her in the cramped space. Even though her heart was still pounding, she felt snug and safe. King had saved the day.

Sally had almost fallen asleep in the cozy quarters by the time she heard voices calling, "Sally! We give up! Come out!"

She stiffly pushed past King, giving him one more pat.

The other kids looked awfully surprised when she came out of the backyard.

Before she could lose her nerve, she went up to Jeremy and said, "Do you think I could take King for a walk sometime?"

Jeremy said, "Sure, if you want to."

Sally smiled. Was Amanda ever in for a surprise!

Happy Birthday, Ollie

By Jeanette D. Knapp

I asked for a dog. They gave me a cat.

"Happy birthday, Ollie," Mom said.

"Many happy returns," said Pop.

"You are so lucky," said my sister, Kate.

I didn't feel lucky. I told myself, hey, this is what happens when you live in an apartment building where no dogs are allowed but cats are okay.

I guess my feelings showed, because Pop said, "Gee, Ollie, try not to get too down in the dumps. You'll have a dog some day."

"Cats aren't so bad," said Mom.

"And they have nine lives," Kate said.

Maybe so, but all I wanted was a dog with *one* life. "Thanks," I said, feeling rotten. Here I was with my birthday present and acting like a baby. But I just couldn't help it.

The orange cat was looking at me with sad, watery eyes. So I took off the blue bow from around its neck. The cat licked my leg in a friendly way, but I still didn't feel lucky.

The cat wouldn't be able to go places with me. I couldn't teach it tricks, like how to sit up and shake hands or roll over and play dead. Cats were just cats. But a dog would have been a friend, a real pal.

Now, here was the cat, shutting its eyes like window shades, and yawning.

"That cat came from Miss Jelly's Pet Shop," Mom said, smiling.

"Miss Jelly says he's special," said Pop.

I didn't see *special*. I saw *sleepy*. I saw a *job* when Kate said, "Cats need lots of attention. Don't forget to feed him."

"So, Ollie," Mom said, "what will you name him?"

I had no ideas. My brain was riding on empty.

"How about Marmalade?" said Kate. "He looks like Marmalade."

"Maybe." I didn't like the name, but I didn't want to hurt my sister's feelings. For now, *Cat* would have to do.

When they left me alone, I said, "Here, Cat," but the cat kept on sleeping. "Nice, Cat," I said, but all he did was purr. "Food, Cat." That woke him up.

Cat followed me into the kitchen. He rubbed against my leg and said, "Meow!" He could hardly wait to eat. In a hurry, I ripped off a corner of the cat food bag.

Cat ate like a gobbling machine. When he finished, I wadded the scrap of paper, tossed it at the garbage can and missed.

But Cat didn't. He skittered across the floor and took the paper ball in his mouth. Coming over to me, he dropped it at my feet. "Meow!" he called, as if to say, "Throw it again!"

So I did. I threw it a lot. Each time Cat went for it and brought it back. He could even catch it in the air—he was that good.

"Almost as good as a dog," I said, scratching Cat behind the ears. His hair was soft and so long I could hide my fingers in it. Cat rolled on his back and let me scratch his stomach. He closed his eyes and purred.

"But you're not a dog," I said, and walked away. Cat followed me into the hall.

"Here, Cat," I said. He followed me into my bedroom. When I closed the door, he started running in circles, trying to catch his tail. I dangled a long piece of string over his head, and he tried to catch that. Finally, I sat on the floor. Cat climbed onto my lap and started licking my ear. His tongue felt scratchy but nice.

Then I got an idea. Pulling everything out from under my bed, the two of us wiggled under it, me with my shiny blue marble. We started this game. It was kind of silly, but kind of hard, at least for Cat. I'd bat the marble out, Cat would scramble after it and bat it back.

Some time later, Mom, Pop, and Kate came into my room.

"Good news, Ollie!" Pop said.

"Wait till you hear!" said Mom.

Kate said, "Ollie, you're so lucky."

Cat and I crawled out from under the bed as Pop said, "We spoke to Mr. Jenkins, the apartment building superintendent."

Cat climbed onto my lap, curling close and draping his paws over my arm.

Mom continued, "When Mr. Jenkins learned that today is your birthday, and that you wanted a dog, he said, 'that Ollie, he's a very responsible young man—'"

"Ollie," Kate interrupted, "Mr. Jenkins said you can have a dog, right now, right this very minute!"

"It has to be small, apartment-sized," Pop said. "We called Miss Jelly, and she has agreed to exchange the cat for a dog."

"So, what are we waiting for, Ollie?" said Mom. "Let's go to the pet shop."

"What a birthday!" said Kate.

Anyone would say that a cat can't understand English. But just then, Cat slunk to my bedroom door. He turned his head, looking at me with sad, watery eyes, as if to say, "Come on, let's get this over with."

"Wait a minute!" I said. "What if I don't want a dog now?"

"But Ollie," Kate said, "it's your dream come true!"

"So, maybe I changed my mind."

The cat stayed. And now he follows me everywhere. He's learning more tricks every day. But I changed his name. I don't call him Cat anymore. I call him Pal, not only because he likes that, but because he is my best friend in the world.

Magnificent Mary

By Dayton O. Hyde

Magnificent Mary must have been hiding behind the corral gate when the Creator made the rest of the horses pretty.

I first saw her and named her in a feedlot for captured government mustangs, where I was selecting animals for our wild horse sanctuary in the hills of South Dakota.

Shaking my head in disbelief that a horse could be that homely, I put her in an adjoining corral with the mustangs I couldn't use, so I wouldn't have to look at her.

She had a head so long she could have drunk from the bottom of a fifty-five-gallon barrel and still peered out over the lip. Her little pig eyes glinted with meanness, and her Roman nose stuck out so far she could have finished a horse race neck to neck and still won by a yard.

Some draft horse ancestor, escaping into the wild, had bequeathed her the genes for huge. Her hipbones protruded like rafters from her fight-scarred hide and they were white from perching magpies. Her mane and tail had acquired such a collection of cockleburs and tumbleweeds that she rattled with each crooked step. Color? I'm not sure she had any, unless it was the color of dirt.

Rejected time and again from the government's adopt-a-horse program, she'd been around that feedlot for a number of years. In truth, she had learned to rule the feedlot, opening gates at will, traveling about as she pleased, and becoming quite a pest.

I'd done my day's work, separating the horses that would do well running wild and free on the sanctuary. I was looking forward to collapsing on a motel bed when Magnificent Mary ambled over to the corral fence and rubbed her tail on a post.

"You cut that out, Old Ugly!" a cowboy shouted at her. But it was too late. I heard the groan of rotten steel as a section of fence disintegrated into rust and dust.

The rest of the wild horses saw the hole in the fence and thundered through it so fast that in three seconds my horses had joined Mary and the rest of the rejects, and all my labors were undone.

It was midnight before we got the corral rebuilt and the horses sorted once more for the long five-hundred-mile trip. Twice I had to separate the old mare from the keepers. She had a mysterious way of getting through the fence, as though she had made up her mind that she was going to the sanctuary and no gate latch could hold her.

I slammed the trailer door shut on the last of the horses and followed the truck's crimson taillights into the darkness, feeling confident that I would never have to contend with that ridiculous old baggage again. But I didn't reckon on what a mischievous bunch of cowboys would do when my back was turned.

Hours later, we unloaded the truck at the sanctuary. The first animal to charge down the chute was Magnificent Mary herself. The truck was heading on to Montana to pick up a load of sheep. There was no way I could send Mary back to the feedlot.

The rest of the wild horses thundered out of the corrals and up over the rimrocks to freedom on the sanctuary, but not Mary. I guess she'd been in captivity for too long to remember freedom. Instead of following the others, she walked calmly to the rail fence separating us, laid it flat with a shove of her massive chest, and headed over to visit me.

Ambling through my vegetable garden, her big hoofs left craters the size of birdbaths in the sifted soil as she sampled a mouthful of cabbage, pulled up several clusters of carrots, sheared off some sprouting corn, razed a row of radishes, and bare-rooted my new raspberry plants.

Garden demolished, she turned her attention to what I was doing, following me just out of reach as though towed by an invisible lead rope. If I turned to look at her, she'd snort an alarm, storm off in a violent retreat, then follow again meekly enough as soon as my back was turned.

As I climbed a ladder onto the roof of the pump house to put on new shingles, Mary regarded my ascent with casual interest, studying me with just one of her gimlet eyes. Then, forgetting my presence, she backed up to the pump house to service an itch on her knotty tail.

"Hey!" I cried out as the small building lurched and began dancing a jig beneath me. The ground seemed suddenly a long distance away. Sliding down the slippery roof on my stomach, I groped desperately for the ladder with my toes.

There was a sudden snort as Mary, rubbing her nose on the ladder, stuck her head through the rungs, shied violently away, and stampeded sideways down the meadow, dragging the ladder with her.

It was dark and a cold wind was blowing in across the prairies from Wyoming when finally a neighbor happened by to return some tools. I was still huddled on the roof.

"What happened?" he asked, flashing a light on me and retrieving the ladder.

"Wind!" I lied as I shivered uncontrollably. "Biggest old tornado you ever did see! Just picked up the ladder and whirled it off over the meadow."

From somewhere nearby in the darkness, I heard a mare whinny. I knew it was Magnificent Mary laughing at me. Grinning to myself, I borrowed my neighbor's light and went to the shed for a bucket of grain. I knew the old mare and I were going to get along just fine.

Snakes Don't Make Good Pets

By Anita Borgo

"Snakes don't make good pets, Junie Ann." Mom sprawled across the daisies. A butterfly flitted around her red bandanna.

Junie held the snake's head firmly. She felt the delicate skull between her fingers. "There's lots of snakes at Noah's Boas Pet Shop. Why don't you want one for a pet?"

Mom shooed away the monarch and eased to her feet. "Because they're slimy, smelly, and sneaky. Where did my trowel go?"

"You dropped it in the coneflowers," Junie said, gently stroking the smooth yellow stripe down the middle of the snake's back. "The smell's almost gone, and he's not slimy at all. Feel."

"Get that thing away from me." Mom shook the trowel with every word.

Junie backed away. "You're afraid?" The snake's slender body wrapped around her wrist like a striped bracelet. "Little Bit wouldn't hurt you. He's a tiny garter snake."

"Don't name that wretched reptile. Only pets have names." Mom tugged off her muddy garden glove and tenderly bent her fingers. "He's already hurt my hand and smashed my daisies. I bet that serpent was the one eating my petunia plants, too." Mom loaded the shovels, hoe, and rake into the wheelbarrow.

"You hurt your hand when you tripped over the rake and landed in the flower bed. The snake didn't push you." Junie watched as the garter's tongue flicked the air.

"Maybe not, but he hid in the lilies, waited till I was close, and jumped on me."

The only jumping Junie saw was Mom hopping around the hyacinths. It wasn't until she caught the eight-inch slitherer that Mom calmed down.

Junie followed Mom into the garage. She stood

in the doorway with the snake. Mom parked the wheelbarrow in a corner.

"Little Bit . . . I mean the snake wouldn't be a pet," said Junie. "He'd be more like a . . . scientific study."

Mom searched for clippers.

"I'd make notes and sketches like a real scientist."

Mom turned. Even in the dim light, Junie recognized her "I-already-said-no" expression.

"There's probably a whole shelf of snake books at the library I could read."

Mom's shoulders slumped. "You knew you'd convince me with the reading argument didn't you?"

Junie unlaced Little Bit from her wrist. The snake stared with shiny eyes and coiled his strong body around Junie's palm.

"This study takes place in the garage," said Mom.

By evening, a cracked aquarium on a tool bench became Little Bit's home. Junie perched on a stool and watched. In the garden, she had to be quick to catch him. In the tank, he crept along the sides. Not finding a way out, he settled into a corner. Junie opened her notebook and wrote "quieter, not as active."

The garage door creaked open. "Say good night to your scientific study and come inside." Mom rubbed her arms. "It's cool tonight. Spaghetti ought to warm us up."

While Mom drained the noodles, Junie skimmed library books. "Remember how the garter smelled when I picked him up?"

"Who could forget?"

"That's how he escapes. Listen, 'Some snakes drive off predators by releasing a foul-smelling odor.'" Junie put down *Super Snakes*. "He thinks we're enemies."

"Humans *are* his enemy. Cars and mowers kill snakes all the time. What else does it say?"

"'Snakes are cold-blooded animals. They warm and cool themselves by moving into sun and shade.'"

Mom tossed the sauce with the noodles. "He probably moved into my garden to cool off."

"But it's *cold* in the garage. He'll need to crawl under leaves or dirt to keep warm. I'll get some out of the compost pile."

"Dinner's almost ready. Sit down, Junie."

"But, Mom . . ."

"I don't want you poking around out there in the dark. Bring the snake in—but only for tonight."

Junie carried the aquarium into her room. Little Bit was still curled in the corner. During dinner, Mom and Junie read about snakes. They found out that the garter snake ate worms, frogs, and bugs—not petunias. Garters have no outside ears, so Little Bit probably didn't hear Mom scream, but did feel the vibrations when she fell into the daisies. He was a shy snake, not a sneaky one. After thinking about it, Mom agreed that he hadn't jumped toward her, but slithered away from her.

After dinner, Junie read that a snake could lash out his tongue without opening his mouth. Junie and Mom wanted to see for themselves. Junie pulled her chair near the tank. Mom watched from across the room.

When Junie told Mom snakes never blinked, Mom moved closer to stare into the garter's eyes. They didn't sparkle like they had this afternoon.

When Junie found out scientists recognized individual snakes from the pattern of scales on the head, Junie sketched Little Bit's pattern. Mom sat in front of the aquarium and compared the garter with photos from *Our Reptile Friends*.

Mom read. "These remarkable, wild reptiles help maintain balance in nature."

Mom closed the book. "Snakes are interesting. I never thought I'd say this, but I'm glad you're keeping Little Bit."

Junie thought about how quickly Little Bit had slithered through the leaves this afternoon. Now he watched quietly through dull eyes. "I'm not."

"What about your scientific study?" asked Mom.

"I'll study him in the garden. He's a wild creature and needs to be free."

Mom gently tapped on the front of the aquarium. The garter flicked his tongue and stared. "I guess you're right."

Junie easily caught the snake. Mom led the way with a flashlight. The daisies had recovered and shimmered in the moonlight. Junie crouched near the lilies.

"Wait," said Mom softly. She stopped next to Junie, extended one finger, and gently stroked Little Bit's back.

Junie opened her hands and the garter disappeared in the darkness.

"I'll miss Little Bit."

"I will miss him, too. But snakes don't make good pets, Mom."

Pet-Napper Trappers

By Beth Thompson

"Hello, Pet Place Hot Line. This is Cielo speaking. How can we help?" Cielo Lonepine opened the call logbook. In her training class, she'd learned that volunteers for Pet Place, the animal rescue organization in Aspen Grove, had to keep careful records. Helping out at Pet Place meant more than just cuddling lost kittens and finding homes for wiggly pups. And the Hot Line was for animal emergencies, so Cielo wanted to do everything right on her first call.

"Someone's stolen Mickey!" The tearful voice on the line trembled with fear. "He was out in the pasture, and then he was gone!"

"Is Mickey a dog or a cat or . . . ?" Cielo paused. In a farming community like Aspen Grove, people also had ponies and miniature goats and even peacocks as pets.

"He's a dog, part Black Lab, part I don't know what. He's medium in size and his coat is kind of curly," the voice said, "and he's my best friend!"

"Could he have just run away?" Cielo asked. "Have you asked the neighbors?"

"We've looked everywhere! My mom and dad are still out looking, but when Mrs. Webster told me she thought she saw Mickey near this blue truck that was driving around slowly, I called you. She said she heard the driver whistle to a black dog. Mickey's so trusting and friendly, he wouldn't suspect a pet-napper! Please help Mickey!"

Cielo was writing furiously. "We'll try," she said, "but first let me get your name and phone number." The caller was Melinda Cates, a girl at Cielo's school. Cielo knew she wouldn't be playing a prank.

"It looks like there's a buncher out there," she told Nick Willis, the Pet Place director. "I just got a call about a missing dog."

"Was it out near Highway 20?" he asked.

Cielo nodded, and Nick frowned. "That's the second call today from there. Looks like a buncher, all right." Cielo had learned about "bunchers" in the training class. They were unscrupulous people who stole pets in bunches and sold them to dealers or guard dog companies or even to laboratories as test animals. These weren't abandoned animals, either. They were loyal, trusting pets, and that was what made them easy targets. Pets were more obedient than strays.

Cielo couldn't understand animal cruelty. She'd always loved animals, maybe because of the stories her grandfather, Swift Eagle, had told her when she was a little girl—all about Native Americans living at peace with all creatures. It was Swift Eagle who'd given her the name "Cielo," which meant "sky." Her friends called her "CeCe" for short, but Cielo was proud of her Indian name and heritage.

"We've got to stop him, Nick," she said. "Everyone out there has one or two dogs, and there are lots of cats, too!"

"That's why he picked this place," said Nick grimly. "He can make a big haul, unless we catch him!"

"I hope Snow is okay," said Cielo worriedly.

"That's right, *your* family's farm is out there, isn't it?" asked Nick.

Cielo nodded.

Nick hesitated, then asked, "Do you think Snow would be willing to act as 'buncher bait'?" When he saw Cielo's frightened look, he added, "We'd be right there. The police, too. But we need to catch the buncher in the act, so he can't claim he just found some strays."

Cielo hesitated. Then she remembered Swift Eagle telling her about a great leader, Chief Seattle, who'd said long ago that animals were our brothers and all living things were connected. Cielo thought about Melinda and her dog, Mickey, and how she'd feel if someone really did steal Snow.

"We'll do it," she said, "just as long as I can be there, too."

Half an hour later, Cielo was leading Snow out to the field farthest from the Lonepine's house. She told him to stay there as she walked back to the house, glancing at the grove of trees where Nick and the police officers were hiding. Once back in the house, she peered carefully past the curtains.

Snow wandered around, sniffing, probably tracking a gopher. He always found their holes, but he could never catch one. Snow was so busy with his hunt, he didn't notice the blue truck cruising slowly past the field. Then it stopped, and a man got out. He glanced around nervously, then held out his hand with something in it and whistled for the dog. Trustingly, Snow trotted over. Suddenly, another man leaped out of the truck and threw a net over Snow, who struggled and yipped. But it was no use. The men dragged him to the truck.

"Nick! Where are you?" Cielo whispered. What if this plan didn't work? What if Snow became *real* buncher bait! I know I promised I would stay here, thought Cielo, but someone has to save Snow! Just as she started out the door, Nick and the police made their move, stopping the bunchers and freeing Snow from the net.

As the police officers handcuffed the pet-nappers, Snow raced across the field to Cielo, who was running toward him as fast as she could. Chief Seattle had said that without animals there was a "loneliness of the spirit" and now Cielo truly understood his words. Nothing felt quite as good as the softness of Snow's coat and the reassuring roughness of his tongue on her face.

"You saved them, Snow! Mickey and all the other dogs! You did it, you and I!" And Snow shook impatiently, as if to say, "Of course, what did you expect?"

Just Henrietta

By David Lubar

Kevin stepped into the crowded gym, holding tightly to the plastic cage. Many of his friends had come to the school pet show. They'd brought all kinds of pets. The air was filled with barks and meows and chirps. He saw dogs, cats, hamsters, and birds. But no one else had a small, pink cage like his. Kevin wondered what would happen next. This was his first pet show, and he hadn't really been sure whether to bring Henrietta. At the front of the room, Mr. Stringer stepped up to a microphone and said, "Everyone with a pet get in line, please."

There was a bit of confusion as people rushed to be first. Kevin took a place near the back of the line. "I'd like each of you to come up and tell us something special about your pet," Mr. Stringer said.

Special? Kevin began to worry. What could he say about Henrietta? What could you say about any hermit crab? The small creature just scuttled around the bottom of the cage. She spent most of her time curled up in her shell.

"This is my dog, Buster," Danny Mitchell was saying. "He can roll over, fetch, and do a bunch of other tricks." Danny demonstrated some of the tricks. The audience laughed and clapped. Kevin looked in the cage. Henrietta didn't do anything.

Sally Polanski went up next, carrying a parrot. "This is Crackers," she said. "He can say over 100 words. Say something, Crackers."

"Pretty Polly," Crackers said. Then Crackers sang a song.

Kevin reached into the cage and picked up Henrietta. "At least come out," he whispered. It would be really boring to hold up a shell. What could he say? "This is Henrietta. She hides in her shell."

Shannon Dwyer was next, with her cat, Licorice. Kevin felt a bit better; what could be so special about a cat? "This is Licorice," Shannon said. "He plays with string, catches mice, watches television whenever there's a cat or dog on the show, and jumps in my lap when I call him."

Kevin felt a small tickle. Henrietta was poking one tiny feeler out from the shell. Tap, tap, the feeler touched Kevin's hand. He held the shell higher and looked inside. Two eyes on the end of stalks look back at him. "Come out," he whispered. He wondered if there was any kind of trick a hermit crab could do.

One by one, the kids went up and showed their pets. Every pet did something interesting—even Mike Feng's lizard, which could change color, and Tina Cruther's ants, which were building a whole city of tunnels and chambers. Danny Zorn brought a plant as his pet. That would have definitely taken the dull prize, except that the plant could eat flies. All the other kids in the class seemed to think this was absolutely wonderful.

I can't believe it, Kevin thought. *Even a plant does more than Henrietta.*

He was just about to take his turn, a turn he really didn't want to take, when it happened. Afterwards, no one was sure whether it was a dog or cat that got loose first. Whichever, all of a sudden there was a dog chasing a cat being chased by two kids. That scared the parrot, who got loose and flew around the gym. The rest of the animals joined in. One cat climbed right up Mr. Stringer's back and held tightly to his shoulder. There were dogs chasing hamsters, cats chasing rabbits, and one puppy chasing its own tail.

As everything around him turned into total chaos, Kevin felt another small tickle. Henrietta was walking across his open hand. When the crab got close to the edge, Kevin held out his other hand. The crab crossed to it and continued walking.

Slowly, everyone around him sorted things out. The kids got their pets back. It took a while to find Mike Feng's lizard, which had blended into a poster on the wall. Nobody—kids or animals—was hurt.

"Your turn, Kevin," Mr. Stringer said.

Kevin stepped up to the microphone. He took a deep breath. He held up his crab. "This is Henrietta," he said. Kevin paused, staring at all the faces in the crowd. "Henrietta is a hermit crab." Kevin paused again. Then the words just popped into his head. "She may be small and shy, but she sticks with me no matter what. I like her."

Most of the kids laughed and clapped. Some couldn't clap because they had their hands too full trying to control their animals. Kevin looked into the shell again. Henrietta looked back. It must be my imagination, Kevin thought, staring at Henrietta. The crab had almost seemed to wink at him.

THE PUPPY PROBLEM

By Carolyn Bowman

"He's back!" Chelsey shouted.

She and Mrs. O'Mally were in the barnyard, watching Ring, the little beagle, race across the field to them.

"Not again!" said Mrs. O'Mally. "That puppy is nothing but trouble."

Chelsey didn't think so. Ring was running circles around them, barking, "Yap, yap, he-l-loo!" Anyone could see that he was glad to be home.

Home was Mrs. O'Mally's barn. Well, it used to be.

Mrs. O'Mally was a breeder. Chelsey, who lived nearby, was her official helper. Several times a year there were new batches of baby beagles. They were born, cared for, then sold. It was a business, Chelsey understood. But right from the start, things had been different with Ring, the runt of a litter.

"This puppy will be called End O'Maine," Mrs. O'Mally had said, "out of Pickadilly Penny and Pickadilly Double-O-Seven."

For Chelsey, those were names that would appear on a pedigree certificate. They had nothing to do with the puppy who'd had such a hard time being born last, who'd had such a hard time surviving those first days.

"Come on, Ring, you can make it," Chelsey had said. She'd called him Ring, because the only distinguishing mark on his black body was a white ring around his tail. Weaning him away from his mother, Chelsey had mixed warm milk, egg yolk, Karo syrup, and lime water, and coaxed him into drinking it.

She helped him graduate into cereal at five weeks. At six weeks, he had taken his first bite of meat. At seven weeks, Chelsey had added mashed vegetables, and by then, it was too late. She was in love with Ring, and Ring was in love with Chelsey.

And then he was sold.

Now, Chelsey was scratching Ring's warm belly, and Mrs. O'Mally was saying, "You get a leash, I'll get the car. We'll have to take him home again."

Ring's new home was with Mr. MacEwan, who lived in an apartment building in town.

It broke Chelsey's heart to see the look on Ring's face when she attached the leash. But her sadness disappeared when they drove to Mr. MacEwan's apartment building, and Mr. MacEwan said, "No thanks, this isn't the dog for me. This beagle is a wanderer. He'll never do."

And so Mrs. O'Mally and Chelsey brought Ring back to the farm.

"We'll have to find another buyer," Mrs. O'Mally said. "For now, take Ring into the barn and give him back to his mother."

Chelsey knew that Mrs. O'Mally cared about her dogs. The woman wanted them to have good homes and eventually she would find one for Ring. She did.

But . . .

"He's back!" Chelsey shouted, and Mrs. O'Mally said, "Not again!"

This time Ring ran away from Mrs. Jones, who managed a day-care center.

Then, "He's back!" Chelsey shouted, and Mrs. O'Mally said, "Again!"

This time Ring ran away from Mr. Lee, who owned a Chinese Restaurant.

Then, "He's back!" Chelsey shouted, and Mrs. O'Mally said, "Again?"

This time Ring ran away from Miss Lupiano, who worked at the bank.

Finally, Ring had a reputation, and no one wanted to buy him.

Well, almost no one.

The following Saturday, Chelsey carried her piggy bank over to Mrs. O'Mally's barn. There was the breeder, serving breakfast to the Pickadilly puppy and saying, "You're not worth two wooden nickels, Ring, but you're the best beagle I own."

This was true, Chelsey knew. Ring was growing into his colors, showing the expected tan, black, and white markings of a beagle. His lines were clean, and he stood proud and straight-backed.

But to Chelsey, Ring was more than a prized beagle. He was a friend, and it was time to help him out. As Chelsey poured the contents of her piggy bank on the ground, the puppy barked, "Yap, yap, he-l-loo!"

Chelsey let the beagle lick her face, then she said, "This money's a down payment. I'll give up my wages until I pay for Ring, in full."

Mrs. O'Mally smiled at the small fortune piled on

the ground. "Why not?" she said. "Ring couldn't have a better master. And if he runs away again, at least we won't have to take him home."

It was a good bargain for all. Mrs. O'Mally won the promise of another line of puppies from Ring. Ring had the home he wanted. And Chelsey? Chelsey had Ring, the best dog in the world.

The Lonely Donkey

By Ann Bixby Herold

A small, gray donkey lived in the meadow down the hill from Nancy Fletcher's new home. The family owned a cat, and Nancy had two goldfish called Flip and Flop, but from the first moment she saw the donkey, she wished it were hers.

On the way home from school with her brother, Tom, she often stopped to give the donkey carrot sticks and apple cores leftover from lunch. When they talked to her and stroked her soft, white nose, the animal's tall, furry ears turned this way and that, so they knew she was listening.

"I wish she were mine," Nancy told Tom.

Tom nodded. "Somebody at school said she belongs to a man called Old Ben who lives in that house back there."

With thick vines covering the walls and winding around the chimneys, the house looked as if it had grown out of the ground.

Hardly anyone ever saw Old Ben, and he spoke so seldom his voice creaked, like an ancient door that needs oiling.

"I don't like folks pesterin' me," he told Nancy when she went with Tom to ask permission to ride the donkey. Up close, he seemed as old as the tree that sheltered his front door. Bright blue eyes stared at them out of a nut-brown face, unfriendly eyes that sent them scurrying away down the overgrown driveway.

One wet autumn afternoon, on their way into town, the Fletcher family passed the donkey on the road. She was pulling a small cart through the puddles, rainwater streaming down her sides. Old Ben sat huddled beneath a waterproof cape, raindrops dripping from the end of his nose.

"We offered to drive him," Mr. Fletcher announced. "He said no. Some people just like to be left alone."

"I don't," said Tom. "I like friends."

"So does the donkey," said Nancy. "She likes me."

"And me," said Tom.

"She likes me best," Nancy argued. "I wish she were mine. She needs somebody to love her."

At Thanksgiving, the family filled a basket with carrots and celery tops, and piled roast turkey on a plate. When they walked up the driveway, the donkey kept pace on the other side of the fence.

Old Ben was chopping wood. He took the plate and nodded his thanks.

"We brought these for your donkey." Nancy held out the basket. "What do you call her?"

He frowned. "Jennet," he said, and he went into the house and closed the door.

Jennet came running when they called her name. As she chewed a handful of celery, she stared at them with her great dark eyes.

"You like me, don't you, Jennet." Nancy slid an arm around her neck.

Jennet tossed her head.

"Me too?" Tom asked, and the donkey tossed her head again.

"There is nowhere for her to shelter out here," Nancy worried.

"He has a shed for his cart," Tom pointed out. "How can he be so mean?"

The weather grew colder. Every day around sunset, down in the meadow, Jennet lifted her head and brayed. Cozy in their warm house, the children could hear her clearly.

The harsh, mournful sounds made them feel so bad they decided to take her a snack each morning on their way to school.

The Christmas vacation came and with it the first snow. Nancy and Tom helped clear Old Ben's driveway. Jennet waded through the drifts to see if they had anything in their pockets.

"She would starve if it weren't for us!" Nancy cried out angrily one day.

"Or die of cold," said Tom.

"Look at her thick winter coat," said their father. "You can tell she is used to living outside."

"Then why does she cry every night?" Nancy demanded.

He had no answer.

Sledding on a nearby hill that afternoon, the children could see Jennet sheltering under a bare maple tree.

It was snowing when they headed home, great soft flakes that blotted out the view. Down in the meadow, Jennet began to bray.

Tears froze on Nancy's eyelashes. "Let's not wait until Christmas, Tom. Let's fill a basket tonight."

The braying had stopped by the time they set off. The moon was out, turning the world from white to silver. In the hush, the only sound was the crunch of their boots on snow.

The meadow was empty. Jennet's hoofprints had disappeared under the fresh snowfall. There was no sign she had ever been there.

They searched and searched, wading through drifts, slipping on icy patches. They looked behind the woodpile, and peered into the cart shed.

"Where can she be?" Nancy's desperate cry left puffs of white hanging in the icy air.

"Look!" Tom whispered.

Snowy hoofprints led across the porch and up to the front door.

Light spilled from a nearby window. The children crept closer.

The room was lit by firelight. Old Ben sat to one side of the hearth, wrapped in a tartan blanket. On the other side stood Jennet. Her eyes were closed, and wisps of steam rose from her coat.

Old Ben was bent over something in his lap. A knife flashed in the dim light, and wood shavings fell to the floor. He scooped some up and tossed them on the fire.

Flames leaped up, brightening the shadowy room. On a table they could see a supper tray. On the hearth in front of Jennet, two round turnips lay nestled in a bed of hay.

Nancy and Tom tiptoed across the porch. They knocked and dropped the basket on the doorstep and ran.

Breathless with cold and laughter, both wanting to be first with the news, they slipped and slid their way home.

On Christmas morning the basket was back on their own step. In it, wrapped together in an old, red flannel shirt, were two small donkeys, carved out of wood.

And a note.

It said, in shaky handwriting:

I am old. If anything happens to me, I want Nancy and Tom Fletcher to have my donkey, Jennet.

Ben Stout

Midnight,
the
Halloween Cat

By Edith Gaines

Kyle had a secret. Mrs. Taylor, his teacher, had whispered it to him when he was helping her mix the paints before school started. Kyle sang a little song to himself while he painted a big orange jack-o'-lantern on his paper. He was so excited that he almost told his friend Mark while they were washing out their paintbrushes.

"Hurry, Mark," said Kyle. "Mrs. Taylor's waiting for us."

"Hurry, Tanya," said Kyle as he hurried across the room to the story corner.

"Move over, Lisa," Kyle said as he slid into an empty space on the floor.

Mrs. Taylor smiled and winked at Kyle. Kyle smiled back. "Sh-h, Lisa," he said. "Mrs. Taylor's got a surprise for us!"

"Indeed I do have a surprise for you. The boys and girls in Mr. Richardson's room have invited us to a Halloween party tomorrow!"

Such excitement! Lisa, Mark, and all the others clapped and giggled. Kyle felt very important since he had kept the secret all morning and hadn't even told Mark.

"What can we bring to the party?" Mrs. Taylor asked. Lisa suggested making popcorn. Mark said that each child could make a mask to wear.

"We need a witch," said Tanya.

Mrs. Taylor laughed. "Should I be the witch? I could take a broom to ride." Kyle and Mark laughed hard, thinking about Mrs. Taylor riding a broom.

"We need a black cat, too," said Kyle. "I can bring a *real* black cat to the party."

Several children shook their heads.

"But he might scratch," objected Lisa.

"Black cats are bad luck," said Mark.

"They're ugly, too," added Tanya.

Kyle felt sad and angry. How could they say such bad things about his beautiful cat?

"Midnight is *not* ugly," he burst out. "She's got fur as soft as velvet. She's a good-luck cat, and she's smart. She can do tricks no other cat can do!"

Mrs. Taylor looked at Kyle. "Midnight does sound like a beautiful cat," she said. "Black cats belong with Halloween. I never heard of a Halloween cat bringing bad luck, did you?"

"No," said the children—all but Mark. The sad look left Kyle's face.

"Could you paint us a big picture of Midnight for the party, Kyle?" Mrs. Taylor asked.

Kyle looked disappointed. "I want the kids to see Midnight *for real*," he said. "She can do tricks for the party."

"I don't know—" said Mrs. Taylor, hesitating.

"Let Kyle bring her," said Lisa.

Kyle promised to bring a leash for Midnight, so she couldn't run around the classroom. Mrs. Taylor decided it would be all right for Midnight to come if Kyle had her on a leash.

After lunch the next day, Mrs. Taylor's room was the busiest place in the whole school. Kyle peeked in from the coatroom door and saw Mark helping two kids finish their funny-face masks. Lisa was popping corn, and Tanya was making a witch's hat for Mrs. Taylor.

"Kyle, where's your cat?" asked Tanya.

"I've got her right here," Kyle said. The children crowded around, while Kyle held the leash.

"She's the biggest cat I ever saw," said Mark.

"She *is* pretty, just like velvet," admitted Tanya.

But Lisa frowned. "I don't believe she can do any tricks," she said.

"Just wait and see," was all Kyle would say.

Soon it was time for the party. A parade of Halloween creatures marched from Mrs. Taylor's room to Mr. Richardson's room. First was a tall witch in a black hat and riding on a broom. Then came all kinds of funny faces with legs and arms that seemed to belong to boys and girls. Two of them carried big pans of popcorn. At the end of the procession was a two-legged cat with a black cat face. His front paw held a leash and behind him trotted a real black cat, wearing a ruffled collar. She was the biggest, most beautiful cat any of the boys and girls in Mr. Richardson's room had ever seen.

When all of the creatures in funny faces found places to sit, the witch waved her broomstick and said in a strange, croaking voice, "We're glad to be here at your party, and we have some special Halloween tricks for you. May I present Kyle and his Halloween cat, Midnight."

The two-legged cat bowed to the audience, still

holding tight to the leash. Then Kyle dangled a little ball of yarn in front of Midnight, just out of her
reach. The cat jumped and swung at the ball, hit-
ting it with a front paw. The children laughed and
clapped. The two-legged cat held the ball higher.
This time Midnight reared on her hind feet and
again hit the ball with her paw. Next the witch
held the broomstick between Midnight and the
dangling ball. Midnight made a flying leap right
over the broomstick.

"Now," said the two-legged cat, "Midnight will
do the greatest trick of all!" He led the big black
cat over to the door and held a pan of cat food just
out of her reach. Then he set the food out in the
hall and closed the door. Midnight sniffed at the
door. She put out a paw and pushed, but the door
was latched so she couldn't open it that way. Mr.
Richardson's class and their funny-face guests all
watched breathlessly as Midnight reared up on her
hind legs again, stretched out her front paws—and
turned the doorknob! Then she pushed against the
door, and this time it opened. The audience clapped
and shouted, "Hooray for Midnight!"

From behind his black-cat face, Kyle shouted,
"Hooray!" too. No one would ever call Midnight an
ugly black cat again.

What Do You Name a Horse?

By Ettie Hunter

What do you name a horse?

That was Jenny Brent's problem, her wonderful problem. For a week she had thought about it and talked about it. Now it was Friday. Tomorrow night, for the first time, she would be riding her own horse in the "showdeo," the children's rodeo and horse show held once a month in Mr. Bill's arena. Jenny wanted her horse to have a name before the show.

For a long time her baby-sitting fees, allowance, and special-jobs money had gone to Mr. Bill's Stables—Western Horses and Ponies Rented,

Bought, Sold, Boarded. Jenny had rented horses, but now she owned one.

It was a small bay mare, just tall enough to be classed as a horse, not a pony. Jenny and Mr. Bill agreed on that point. They also agreed that she was part quarter horse and, like most quarter horses, would be quick to respond to a rider's instructions.

On the half-door of her stall was the poster Jenny's brother Joe had printed and tacked up on her eleventh birthday. It read:

> **Happy Birthday from Your Family. You only have to name her.**

Only!

In the covered runway before the long row of stalls, Jenny appealed to Mr. Bill. "I have to pick some kind of name for her before tomorrow night," she moaned.

Mr. Bill leaned against the tack room door, waiting for Jenny to adjust a brightly colored saddle blanket before he helped her lift the western saddle in place.

"Keep it short, Jenny" he said. "Don't pick anything long or fancy. She came from Texas.

Texas is a big name for a small horse, but you could put Little in front of it. Little Texas. What do you think of that for a name?"

Jenny thought about how "Little Texas" sounded as she rode into the arena at the end of the runway. Mr. Bill's daughter Reba was waiting to help her practice the reining pattern that was one of the show's events. It was hard for Jenny to believe that she had a horse who seemed to know exactly what to do after the run-in—stop, settle, figure-eights, pivots, roll-backs, and walk to the judge. Reba pretended to be the judge. She handed Jenny a wisp of hay as a make-believe ribbon and stroked the mare's red-brown neck.

"She's so good at this, I wonder how long she's been doing it?" she asked.

Afterward the girls used a currycomb and body-brush until the mare's coat looked like wet plastic. Reba suggested a name.

"You got this horse on Monday. Why don't you name her Monday? It would be like Robinson Crusoe's man Friday."

Just then Reba's brother, a veterinarian called Dr. Dave, came out of a stall. He had been doctoring a colt that had been a bit too friendly with a barbed wire fence.

"Seeing you girls polish that horse gives me a

name idea," he said. "You've heard the saying: 'Short horse, soon curried.' Let's call this one Shorty. It suits."

"She isn't that short," answered Reba, "and Shorty has a pony sound."

When Joe came to take his sister home, he had a suggestion, too.

"If you say one more time that you'll name your horse tomorrow, I'll believe you and call her Tomorrow. Why don't you name her Today? It's shorter."

At the supper table Joe repeated his suggestion. Everyone laughed, but Mrs. Brent said, "Stop teasing, Joe. Try to help." She turned to Jenny. "Did you ever think of using her color? There was a quarter horse named Yellow Jacket. You could call her Brown Bee."

"No," Jenny shook her head. "I don't want to name her after an insect.

"I wonder what she was called before?" Jenny's dad asked. "Maybe you could find out. Wouldn't you be confused if, after eleven years of being Jenny, you had to answer to Dorothy Lavinia?"

Two people at the supper table made no suggestions. Julie, Jenny's baby sister, banged on her highchair and chanted, "Nice horsie! Nice horsie!"

Jenny knew that Julie was right, but "Nice Horsie" was not a name.

The other person was Jenny's grandmother. She laughed at Joe's joke, smiled at Julie's chant, and patted Jenny's hand.

"I'm sure you'll think of the right name by tomorrow," she said. "I'll take you out in the morning for a last practice. And tomorrow night I'll be there when the announcer says '. . . and Jenny Brent riding . . .'"

"Jenny Brent riding Today," interrupted Joe.

"Now, Joe," said Gran.

But on the way to Mr. Bill's the next morning, Jenny admitted that she was still searching for a good name.

"Isn't it silly, Gran?" she asked. "When a girl has wanted a horse forever—well, at least for three years—she should be able to think of a name when she finally gets one. I don't know why I'm so hard to suit, but I am."

"I think I know why," said Gran, bringing her car to a stop in the stable driveway. Beyond the gate they could see that the runway was full of children and horses. They were getting ready for the show.

"Your horse is special. You want a just-right, special name. You don't want it to be funny. You don't want it to be too unusual. When people speak of Jenny's horse you really want them to mean your special pride and joy. It's the same thing I want people to mean when they say 'your granddaughter.' You see, you're my pride and joy, Jenny."

Instead of getting out of the car, Jenny sat thoughtfully fingering her long brown hair and staring at her grandmother. Suddenly, she reached over and hugged her.

"Oh, Gran, you've done it! You have named my horse."

Grand looked startled. "I have?" she asked. "What do you mean?"

"It's right—what you just said about my name and pride and joy. Jenny's Joy! It'll please everybody who wanted a short name. And it's different, but not too much so."

Jenny jumped out of the car, her long hair flying. She turned and leaned on the car door, smiling at her grandmother.

"You do like it, don't you, Gran?" she asked.

Gran smiled back. "Of course I do. If you like the name, I like the name. The difference is that you like the Joy part best, but I like the Jenny part." She turned the car key. "Now, run! The way you tell it, the Jenny part needs lots of practice before the show, even if the Joy part doesn't. And I want to be proud of both."

Dorsey Delivers the Mail

By Elizabeth Van Steenwyk

Dorsey waited patiently while the postmaster fastened the mailbag to him. One strap went under his stomach, the other around his chest.

"Good dog," the postmaster said, when he had finished. "Now you're all ready for your route to East Calico. But be careful today, fella. There are robbers working the hills on your route. If you see them, run as fast as you can."

The postmaster didn't expect the small brown-and-white collie to understand him. But sometimes

73

the collie seemed as if he did. Nevertheless, it was good advice to hear. This was the mid-1880s, a time when the West was still being settled, a time when lawmen were few and lawbreakers were many.

Dorsey's owner, Mr. Stacy, had moved to Calico, California, to mine for silver. But the town grew quickly to a population of three thousand and Mr. Stacy felt crowded. He moved to East Calico, a smaller town up in the hills. Only about forty people lived there.

But Dorsey missed his old friends back in Calico so he walked back down the trail often to see them. In fact, he walked back almost every day. Finally someone got an idea. Why not teach Dorsey to deliver the mail? The postmaster and Mr. Stacy rewarded him with loving hugs and bites of good things to eat so it didn't take Dorsey long to learn his job. Soon he carried the mail in a special bag attached to him and his collar.

Each day, after Dorsey had the mailbag attached to him, he walked along the dusty streets of Calico on his way out of town. But first he had to say hello to all his friends. He stopped at the blacksmith shop. The blacksmith was busy at his forge, making shoes for a horse, but he gave Dorsey a friendly pat. Then Dorsey moved on to the General Store where he barked a good morning to the owner. Next he stopped at the boardinghouse and restaurant for a bit of breakfast. Finally, he trotted into the one-room schoolhouse. The children stopped their lessons to call a greeting to him.

Now Dorsey was ready for the walk up the trail to East Calico. Today there were no sandstorms, no winter snows, or blistering heat through which he had to walk. Today there was only the beauty of the surrounding mountains. All the colorful rock formations had reminded the town's founders of a bright fabric called calico, so they named their town for it. Warm sun shining on early spring wild flowers made the route even more pleasant. If there were robbers nearby, they didn't bother Dorsey.

It didn't take him long. Soon he arrived in East Calico and delivered the bag of mail to lonely prospectors who hoped for a word from home. Then Dorsey went to his home with Mr. Stacy, received his reward and rested up until the next day. This had been another successful delivery. He hadn't lost a single piece of mail.

Dorsey was very faithful as the days went by. Sometimes the miners tried to distract him. They played pranks on him but he simply hid in the bushes or behind rocks until the pranksters gave up and went away. Dorsey was a faithful worker and let nothing disturb him from his route.

One day the postmaster in Calico received a box addressed to a miner who lived in East Calico. The miner's mother had made some candy to be delivered to her son. So the postmaster strapped the box to Dorsey's back with the other mail and sent him on his way.

Except, the candy never got there. When Dorsey arrived with the mail in East Calico, the box was still strapped to him, but it was empty. A corner of the box was torn open, and the candy was gone. No one knew what happened. Had Dorsey smelled it, ripped the box open, and eaten the candy to satisfy his hunger? Or, had someone caught him and become curious, ripped open the box, and couldn't resist the homemade sweets? Or, did Dorsey bump up against a jagged rock and rip the box open accidentally?

It was the only time Dorsey failed to deliver in his long career. No one got mad at Dorsey, though. People just wished he could talk so he could tell them what had happened.

Finally, Dorsey grew too old to deliver the mail, and he retired. A man who lived in San Francisco adopted him and gave him a good home for the rest of his days.

The town of Calico was restored in the 1950s when Walter Knott of Knott's Berry Farm bought it.

Mr. Knott had sentimental reasons for doing this. He once had worked in the mining town back in 1910 when he first came to California. Dorsey's tale is now told to visitors who come to Calico Ghost Town located just off Highway 15 on the California desert, not far from Barstow. Dorsey's story always inspires questions from those who hear it. But one question still remains. Whatever happened to the box of homemade candy? No one will ever know.

STUCK
IN
NEUTRAL

By Cris Peterson

"Get off my foot, you big oaf!" Jerry shouted. His 500-pound Holstein calf rolled her eyes as she chewed her cud. All four hoofs stayed put.

Jerry threw down the calf's halter. "Move," he said as he shoved the stubborn animal. The calf sidestepped an inch or two. Every bone in Jerry's foot felt crunched.

Just then, Jerry's older brother, Brent, climbed down from the hayloft. "Having trouble with Clover? Sounds like a riot." Crossing his arms, Brent leaned against a post near the door. "She'll never be ready in time for the fair."

"Yes she will!" Jerry shot back. But he wasn't as sure as he sounded.

Jerry bent to check on his toes. *Brent's right,* he thought. *I'll never win a blue ribbon like he did last year. I don't have a chance.*

Jerry limped to the gate and swung it open. "Come on, girl." He tugged on the halter.

Clover's legs locked in place.

"You'll have to build a fire under her," Brent said. "She's stuck in neutral."

"Don't just stand there. Help me push her!" Jerry shouted. He jerked the halter in frustration. "I might as well quit!"

Brent shoulder-blocked the calf from behind. Clover stumbled out the barn door and scuffled down the driveway behind Jerry.

For months, Jerry had practiced leading Clover. But during the past week she seemed to have forgotten everything. It couldn't have happened at a worse time. Jerry's first cattle show was tomorrow.

Jerry's stomach felt as heavy as a pail of rocks when he thought about the show. Everyone would laugh at him and his stubborn calf.

A tug on the halter broke in on Jerry's thoughts. Clover was kneeling in the gravel.

"You're impossible," Jerry said with a sigh. After five minutes of pulling and tugging, Clover finally heaved herself up. Jerry struggled to lead her back to the barn.

The next morning Jerry woke with a start. He had tossed and turned and worried half the night. After the way she had acted yesterday, Clover would be a disaster.

"Do I really have to do this?" he asked Dad on the way to the fairgrounds. "Clover doesn't want to lead at all."

"We talked about this earlier," Dad said. "Clover is a beautiful calf. If you stay calm you'll do fine."

Minutes later, Jerry and Brent led their calves out of the trailer and walked them to their stalls. Brent tied his calf and took off with friends, leaving Jerry by himself.

Jerry shook out some straw, and Clover settled into the bedding. Jerry plopped down on a hay bale next to her. "Please, girl," he said. "Give me a break and lead like a good calf."

Clover flipped at the flies with her tail and chewed her cud.

"Giving her some last-minute instructions?" Brent asked when he returned. "The whole cattle club is here. We'll cheer you on."

Jerry gulped and grabbed the currycomb.

"Great," he thought as he brushed the calf. "Everybody will see me make a fool of myself."

The hours before the show evaporated. As he waited to lead Clover into the arena, Jerry scanned the bleachers. He recognized almost everyone. His knees shook. It was hard to swallow. The Holstein calf class was already under way.

"Numbers 12 through 18 are up next," blared a voice from the loudspeaker. Clover shied away from the sound.

Jerry pulled Clover into the ring. "Keep your eyes on the judge," he told himself. "Keep her head up. Stay calm."

Clover plodded through the ankle-deep sawdust, her eyes bulging. The hot, dusty air burned Jerry's throat. He glanced at Brent and Dad, seated in the front row. Dad smiled, and Brent surprised Jerry by giving him a thumbs-up sign.

Jerry and Clover circled the ring several times, and Jerry began to relax a little. *Maybe we'll be OK,* he thought.

Suddenly he felt a tug on the halter. Clover was kneeling in the sawdust! Jerry snapped the halter up, forcing her to struggle to her feet. Jerry glanced at the judge. "Oh no," he thought, "he saw it all." Jerry felt the blood rush into his face and knew he must be as red as a stop sign.

"Line them up," the judge called. He motioned Jerry into place at the end of the line.

Gritting his teeth, Jerry set up his calf in front of the judge. "Last," he thought. "We finished last." He wanted to bury himself in the sawdust.

Clover stood perfectly still. Bits of sawdust clung to her knees.

The judge spoke into a microphone. "Our first-place winner today has obviously spent many hours working with his calf. This calf has more strength than the others, and the exhibitor showed good control when the animal tried to lie down."

Jerry's heart stopped as he was awarded the prize. He stared at the blue ribbon in disbelief. The judge directed him to circle the arena a final time on his way out. Everyone applauded.

Brent and Dad met him at the arena gate. "Way to go," Dad said. "You did a great job."

"Boy, I thought I was the loser," Jerry said. He hugged Clover around the neck.

Brent slapped him on the back. "A blue-ribbon loser! You can't beat that."

THERE'S A
DOG
IN THE
OVEN!

By Monte G. Snyder

Uggy couldn't wait to see what all the commotion was about. From the backyard she heard a large truck and strange voices moving something into the house. Maybe it was a new bed, Uggy thought. Her old one by the fireplace was a little worn out.

After the truck had left, Jeffrey, her twelve-year-old owner, let her into the house. Uggy carefully sniffed each corner as she went through the pantry toward the kitchen. From the kitchen she could see that her dog dish and bed were still in their places. Then she spied a large white object in the corner of the kitchen.

Uggy knew it was her duty to protect the family, so she barked a warning at Jeffrey and cautiously smelled the strange intruder. To her surprise, Jeffrey patted her head and said, "It's all right, girl. It's just our new stove."

Uggy sniffed, her nose touching the cool enameled metal and the shiny trim. First she sniffed each corner and underneath, then as high as she could on the reflecting glass in the door panel.

"That's the oven," said Jeffrey. Suddenly Uggy jumped back and growled in surprise.

There was a dog in the oven! She had seen it with her own eyes! This would certainly take some getting used to.

Uggy couldn't hear or smell a dog, but every time she looked in the oven window, there it was, staring back at her.

Why did the Martin family need another dog? she wondered. Everyone knew Uggy was the most perfect dog anyone could possibly have. She barked furiously at strangers, always stayed quiet when Jeffrey's father was napping, played fetch for hours, and even chased those pesky birds and squirrels from the backyard.

Now that there was a new dog, Uggy would have to try twice as hard to be the world's best pet.

That night Jeffrey's mother prepared a big dinner. The clatter of dishes and the smell of food drifted from the kitchen. It made Uggy hungry and curious. Uggy was never allowed in the kitchen while Jeffrey's mother cooked, but tonight the smell of meat, bread, and buttery vegetables was almost too much for a dog to resist.

When no one was looking, Uggy left her bed and crept across the living room carpet. She could hardly keep from running in and helping herself to dinner, an action very unlike the world's best pet. Instead, Uggy crept the last few inches to a spot where she could see right into the kitchen. There, she received her second shock of the day.

Jeffrey's mother had just opened the oven. But instead of seeing the new dog jump out, Uggy spotted a large, steaming, covered pan. And from the pan came the familiar smell of meat.

Uggy crept backwards. Then she ran to the safety of her bed. *Could this be the end of the dog in the oven?* she wondered.

Thinking about the poor dog, Uggy couldn't eat her own dinner. The laughter coming from the dining room only made her feel worse. Uggy didn't want another dog around the house, but she wouldn't wish what had happened on even her worst enemy!

Before long, Uggy actually began to miss the dog in the oven. She thought of the games they could have played, and how nice it would have been to share her watchdog responsibilities. By the time dinner was over, Uggy would have given anything to have her new friend back.

The next morning Jeffrey called Uggy outside to play. Uggy could smell the warm air and hear the noisy birds that needed chasing. But she didn't feel very playful. She rose and stretched, smelled her leftover dinner, and headed toward the backyard. She slowed as she entered the kitchen.

Uggy found it hard to look at the oven, so she stared at the linoleum and her feet. *This is where my friend lived until last night,* she thought to herself.

Outside, a car door banged shut. Uggy jerked her head up at the noise. She found herself looking directly into the oven window. Uggy couldn't believe her eyes! Someone was staring back at her.

Uggy yelped and ran in circles. She stopped and gave the oven a slurpy lick, then dashed outside to tell Jeffrey the good news.

Uggy whirled at Jeffrey's feet, barking furiously for him to follow. She tugged on Jeffrey's striped shirt with her teeth.

"What's wrong, girl?" Jeffrey asked. They raced indoors to the gleaming oven. Uggy barked at the reflecting glass.

Jeffrey laughed. "It's all right, girl," he said as he knelt down beside Uggy. "That's just your reflection that you see."

Uggy thought Your Reflection was a strange name for a dog, but her old friend was back, and that was all that mattered.

Just as Uggy pressed her nose to the glass for another victory lick, she saw someone kneeling beside her friend. She saw red hair, and a striped shirt that seemed familiar.

Uggy stiffened in surprise. She could hardly believe her eyes. Now there was a *boy* in the oven!

Friends
to the
Rescue

By Patricia White

Kathy and Sue had been best friends for as long as they could remember. They were both in Mr. Duffy's fifth-grade class, and they both took ballet lessons at the Downtown Dance Studio. But the girls' main interest was horses.

Every day after school they were at Mr. Peterson's stable, where they would watch as Carolyn, Mr. Peterson's niece, groomed the two horses, cleaned out their stalls, and polished all the saddles and bridles in the tack room. Kathy and Sue were never happier than when Carolyn let them help her, pushing the wheelbarrow full of soiled straw bedding out to the huge pile in the woods or climbing into the hayloft to throw down the heavy, sweet-smelling bales of hay.

Candy, the bay mare, was Sue's favorite, but Kathy dreamed of riding Duke, the tall, dapple-gray thoroughbred. On Saturdays, after Mr. Peterson had ridden Duke over the jump course, he would let Kathy unsaddle him and walk him until he was cooled down. Kathy often thought about how wonderful it would be to ride Duke herself. But she knew she would never be brave enough to ask.

Late one Saturday afternoon Kathy and Sue were walking home from the library, each carrying the usual armload of horse stories. As they passed Mr. Peterson's, Kathy saw that one of the stable doors was open.

"Oh, Sue, look!" cried Kathy. "Duke's door is open, and it doesn't look as if anyone is home. He must have gotten loose!" The two friends raced toward the barn.

When they reached the stable, the girls were relieved to find Duke standing quietly next to the tack room door. Kathy was about to go inside for a lead strap to take him back to his stall when she realized why the gray gelding had stood so calmly when they had run up to him. The tack room door was open and Duke had his head inside. He had knocked the lid off one of the grain barrels and was helping himself to the oats.

"Look at the mess he's made," exclaimed Sue. "Let's put him back in his stall and clean this up." Sue snapped a lead strap onto Duke's halter and led him back to his stall. In the meantime Kathy picked up the metal lid and was about to put it on the grain barrel. She peered inside and noticed that the container was almost empty.

"What are you staring at?" asked Sue, coming back into the tack room.

"This barrel is almost empty, Sue," said Kathy. Her mind was racing. "Don't you remember reading about horses getting sick when they eat too much grain? It's called colic and they can die from it. Sue, we have to do something!"

"Oh, Kathy, he didn't look sick. He was just having a little snack," Sue said, trying to persuade Kathy to calm down.

But Kathy had already run from the tack room and was opening the door to Duke's stall. The big gray was lying on his side in the straw, making low groaning sounds. When Kathy came in, he climbed to his feet for a moment, but soon he went down again, trying to roll in the straw.

"He sure looks as though he has a tummyache now," Sue said as she came over to her friend.

"Sue, we have to get help!"

Now Sue was beginning to feel frightened. "But no one is home. There's no car in the driveway. What can we do?" Sue asked.

Kathy tried to remember what she had read in the *Horseowner's Handbook* that she had checked out of the library last week. What was the treatment for colic? Then she remembered: *Keep the horse on its feet.* If Duke were to lie down and roll, his intestines could become twisted. That would be dangerous. Duke might even die.

"Run next door, Sue, and call Dr. Baker," Kathy said. "We'll have to walk Duke until the doctor gets here."

Sue ran next door as fast as she could, while Kathy urged Duke to get up. But he just lay there in the straw, his beautiful gray coat breaking out in sweat. She pulled on the lead strap again.

"Please, Duke, you have to get up. Come on, boy!" Kathy pleaded. Just then Duke stretched out his long forelegs and struggled to his feet. Kathy was able to coax him to the door, and they began to walk slowly around the paddock.

Soon Sue came running up the path, trying to catch her breath. "He's coming! He's on his way!"

she shouted. "Dr. Baker says we're to keep walking Duke until he gets here," she added.

On and on the girls walked the sick horse. Every once in a while he would stop and try to lie down, but they were able to keep him moving. It was beginning to get dark when they saw the veterinarian's van pull into the driveway.

Dr. Baker hurried up the path with his large black bag. "OK, girls, bring him into the stable, and we'll see what kind of shape he's in," he called.

Kathy held Duke's lead while Sue passed the doctor's medicine and equipment to him. Soon the treatment was over and Duke was resting comfortably in his own stall.

"You girls did an excellent job," Dr. Baker began. Just then Mr. Peterson's car drove up. Seeing the stable lights on, he came quickly up the path. "Dr. Baker . . . girls . . . what's wrong?" he asked, his voice full of concern.

"Your gray had a touch of colic, Bob. These young ladies did some quick thinking and may have saved his life," Dr. Baker replied.

Without a word Mr. Peterson hurried to Duke's stall. When he saw that Duke would be all right, he turned to Kathy and Sue.

"I don't know how to thank you girls, except to say that I think you'll both make fine horsewomen someday. And as soon as Duke is feeling up to it, I'll make sure you both have a chance to ride him."

Sue looked at Kathy and smiled. She knew her friend's dream was about to come true.